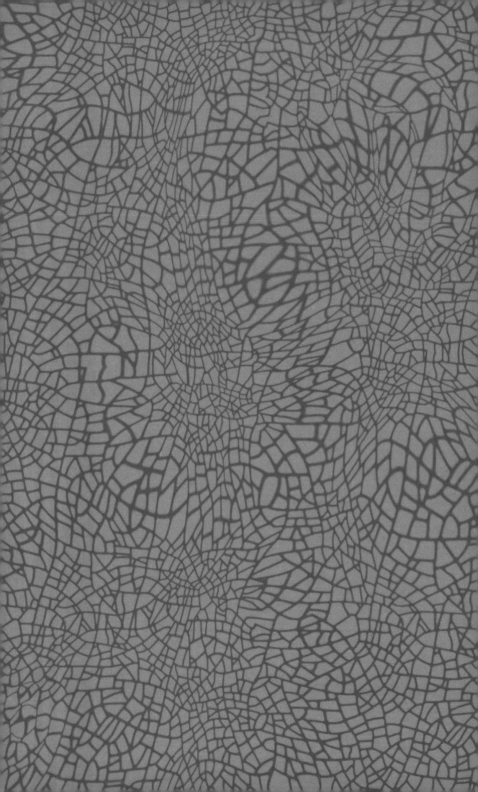

Dinner time

What's this greedy dragon been eating?

Burp!!

Yum!
Yum!

Fill me up...

Phewy!!

15

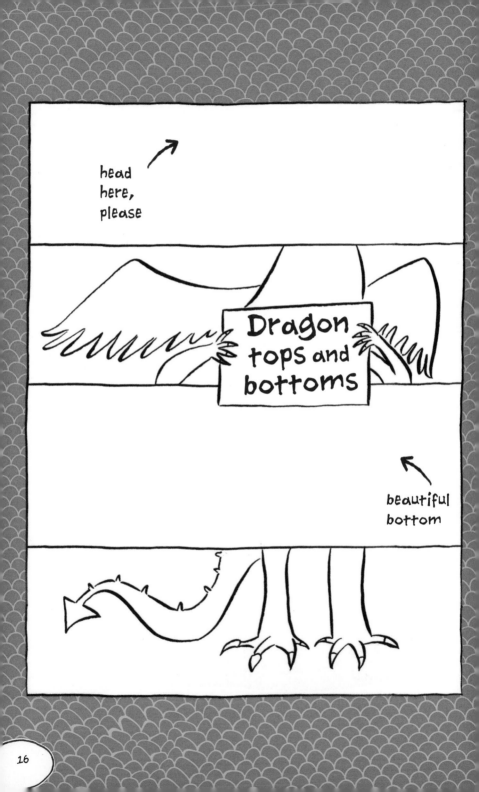

17

The dragon and me

I was lying in bed when suddenly I heard a noise. I opened the curtains and looked out. Good boy! A fire-breathing dragon! "Hop on my back," it said, "I'm taking you for a ride."

I climbed aboard and as I looked down, I could see
... a cat, a bat,
... an elegant owl
... and a fox on the prowl.

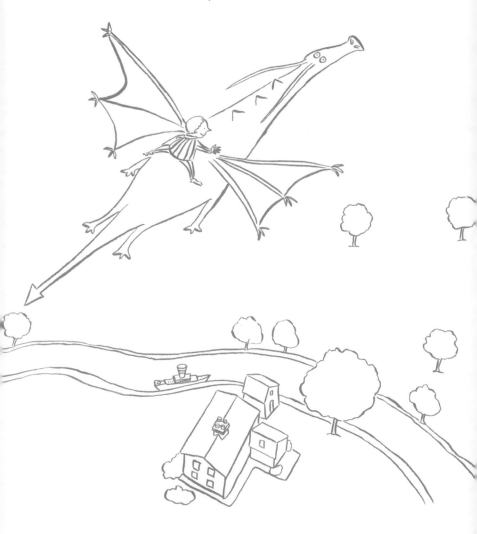

Draw in all the things the little boy could see.

Dragon fashion

Stick some clothes onto these fantastic dragon models.

← T-shirt

hat

gloves

21

What's happening?

Draw something scary!

Why is the silly knight up the tree?

Dragons to the rescue!

Draw more dragons to make a fire engine crew!

Super sticker quiz

Which STICKERS belong in these circles?

Find a fierce BABY with lots of sharp teeth.

Use this to help you fight dragons.

What comes out of a dragon's MOUTH?

I live in MOUNTAINS and I'm not very nice.

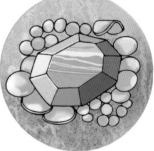

Dragons love these a LOT!

Answers are at the back of the book.

Once upon a dragon time

Make up your own STORY using these pictures...

① ② ③

④

⑤

Draw the ending here.

⑥

...and they lived happily
ever after (or did they?).

27

Seeing double

There are **12** differences.
Can you spot them?

Answers are at the back of the book.

Design your own
coat of arms

draw in
missing deer

decorate shield

write your family motto here

Color in and complete your own
coat of arms.

Decorate the shields and flags using the
pictures below, or make up your own.

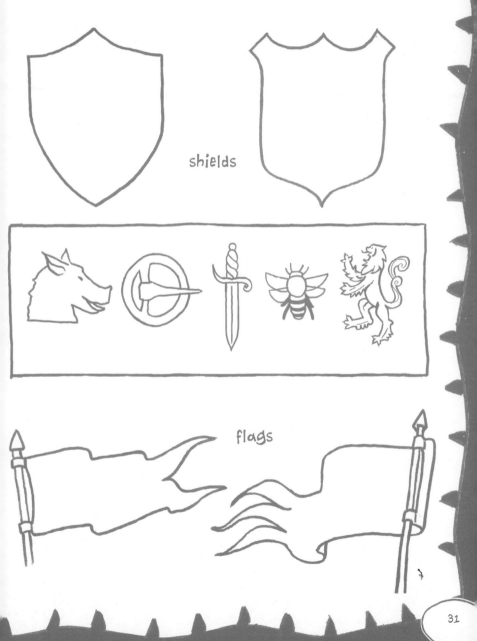

shields

flags

Who lives where?

Why not add a dragon sticker?

Draw some SNOW DRAGONS chilling out in this snowy scene.

Naming knights

What would you be called if
you were a knight?

Take the name of your first pet

....

What is your lucky number?

....

Now add your hometown

....

Arise, Sir ....

(e.g., Tiddles the 27th of Oxford)

It's mine, all mine

Color in the
DRAGON and
its treasure.

Arty adventure!

Why not test your artistic skills by completing the scenes with your colored pencils?

Help! Mad creature attacking the castle!

Who's hiding here? (Clue—he's a baby but still breathes fire.)

What is the knight trying to shoot?

Draw a huge pile of treasure here.

Dragon-taming potions

What's inside the jars?
Draw in some of your own, too.

Pink Sparklebat

Amazonian Firebreath

Scaly Egghead

Egg decorator needed!

Tufted Greyworm

Decorate these dragon EGGS. Use the scaly paper if you like.

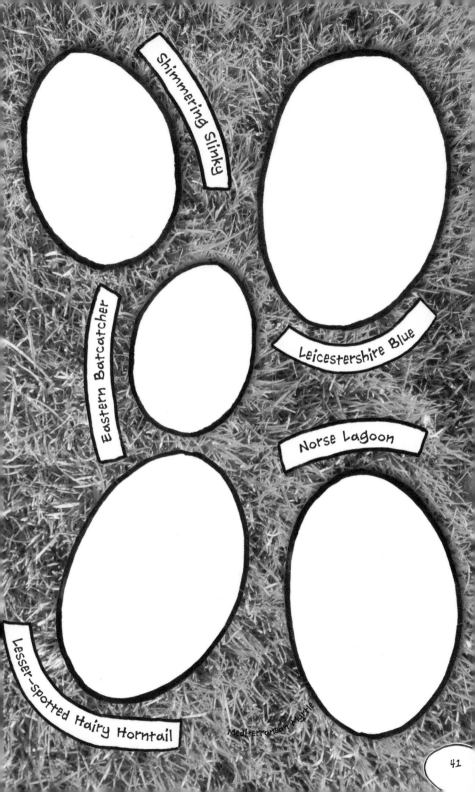

Shimmering Slinky

Eastern Batcatcher

Leicestershire Blue

Norse Lagoon

Lesser-spotted Hairy Horntail

Mediterranean Myrtle

Dragon anatomy

leathery wings
and sharp spines

↓

red hot
flames

↓

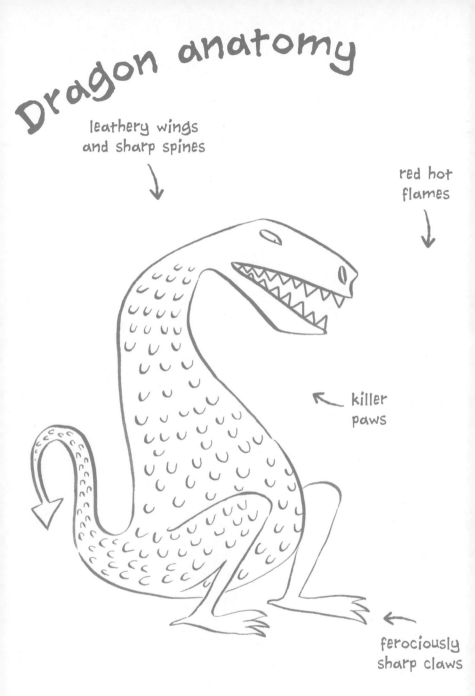

← killer
paws

← ferociously
sharp claws

Draw in the missing BODY parts.

A-mazing

Help the knight find his way through the MAZE without waking the sleeping dragon. Shh!

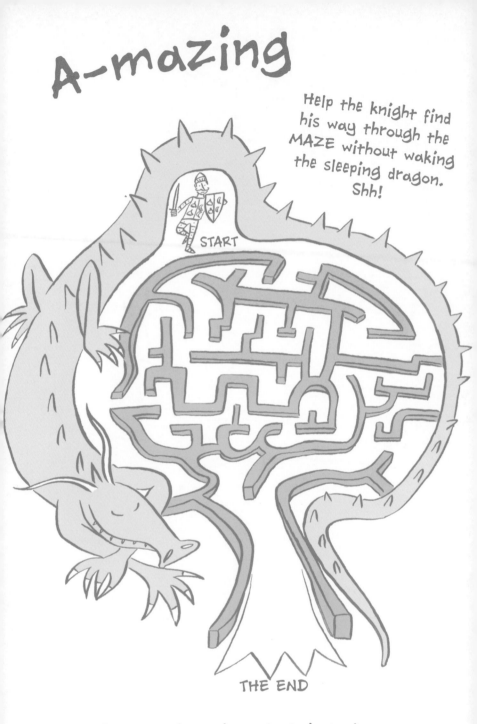

START

THE END

The answer is at the back of the book.

Most hideous and monstrous

Witches like...

_____
_____
_____
_____

Wyverns

are very nasty two-legged

dragons that don't like...

_____
_____
_____

Most sea serpents live in...

_____

_____

_____

Color in and describe these silly creatures.

Ogres like to eat...

_____

_____

_____

_____

_____

45

Eye, eye

Which EYES will you draw on each dragon?

Down at the talon salon

How would you like your NAILS done today?

Count the dragons

Count the dragons in the egg,
then write the number in the box.

The answer is at the
back of the book.

Who's knitting?

Write a name for the dragon here.

Join the dots to find out who's hiding here.

The answer is at the back of the book.

Baby dragons

Who's going walking in the park?

cute dragon twins

naughty older brother

Design a book cover for this

MONSTER bestseller

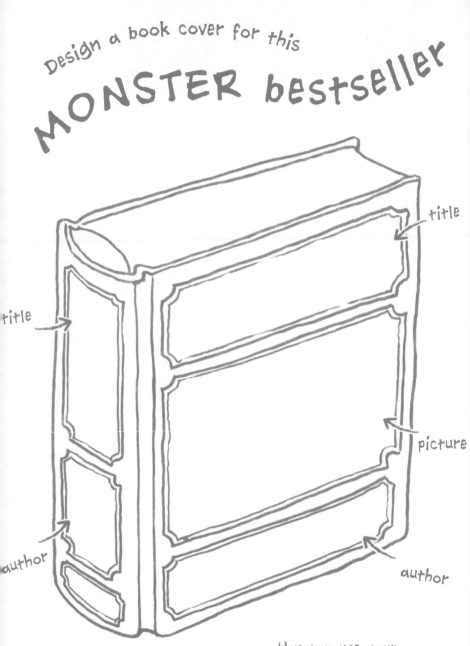

title

title

picture

author

author

You can use your
stickers here, too.

Spot the difference

Can you spot 10 differences between these dragon pictures?

Answers are at the back of the book.

Secret dragon map

Draw a magical dragon map
using the pictures below.

little cottages

deserted
castle

dragon mountains

dark caves

passing sheep

whistling woods

winding river

stepping
stones

X You could draw some hidden treasure!

Flying with dragons

Up, up in the sky, with the dragon I fly...

Draw yourself on the dragon's back.

What are they saying?

Fill in the speech bubbles.

Inside the dragon's castle

Draw something in every room.

The handsome dragon

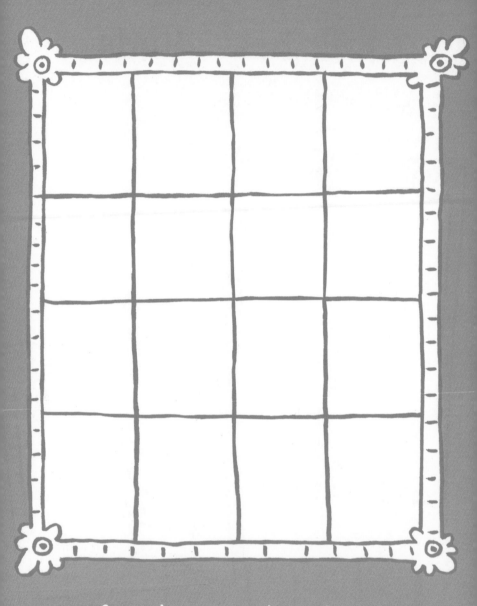

Copy the dragon picture here.
Try drawing one square at a time.

The good knights' guide

Mirror, mirror on the wall, who is the BRAVEST knight of all?

SIR HAVELOT THE HANDSOME

Handsome Sir Havelot is more interested in wooing fair maidens than fighting dragons.

SIR BORIS THE BRAVE

No one has ever seen Sir Boris's face but he is well known for the bright red plume on his helmet.

Read these knights' descriptions and draw in their missing features.

SIR JASPER THE BIG NOSE

Sir Jasper has a very big nose, enormous ears, and goofy teeth. He is, however, a charming knight...

SIR BARRY THE BEARDED

Sir Barry can barely see the dragons he fights due to his gigantic curly beard!

Fantastic beasts

What do you get if you cross a dragon with a poodle? A DRAGON-O-POODLE!

dragon   poodle   dragon-o-poodle

Now it's your turn...

dragon   giraffe

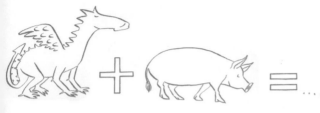 = ...

dragon   pig

  = ...

dragon   horse

 = ...

dragon   duck

Who's flying tonight?

Find the stickers that match these strange nighttime shapes.

Answers are at
back of the book.

Dragon things to color in

cave

dragon

dragon eggs

dragon's tooth

claws

eye

wizard

knight on horse

scales

bones

poison

feathers

jewels

maiden

Wildlife photographer

Draw some wild animals here.

Fire-breathing contest

Help the dragons
light the candle by
drawing in their
fiery flames.

Name that baby!

Puffy

. . . .

. . . .

What do you think these cute baby dragons are called?

. . . .

. . . .

79

Knights and maidens

tops and bottoms

Here are more SCALES for you.
Look back at page 10 for
what to do with them.

Amazing things to do with your

dragon stickers

1 Play with your DRAGON STICKERS over and over again on the sticker pages in the book.

2 Look out for these other pages where you can use your STICKERS:
25, 30-31, 50, 55, 60, 64-65, 72-73, 88, ...and wherever else you like!

3 Use the stickers to decorate your ROOM and the things around you (always ask an adult first).

4 Make your own dragon sticker PICTURES and give them to your friends and family.

Shining armor

Color in this bold knight
and his horse, ready to go
in search of dragons.

Family pictures

Draw in the missing relations for the photo album.

weird

Cousin Bongo Rockers

party animal!

Hotpants Hattie

Uncle Snortgrundler

best to avoid

Mom—on a good day

black sheep

Fast-and-free Freddy

possibly kidnapped

Long-lost brother Bruno

smug

2nd cousin Colin

bonkers

Auntie Ursula

Find the right home

Follow the lines to see where each dragon lives.

Answers are at the back of the book.

Color in the
Dragon words

KNIGHT

EGGS

Fire

TREASURE

serpent

scales

Big squares for dragon doodles

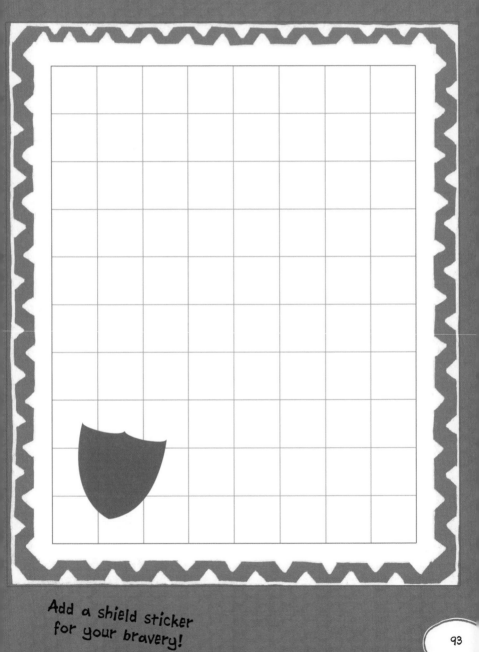

Add a shield sticker
for your bravery!

WANTED

Dead or alive, but preferably dead!

The world's most
DANGEROUS DRAGON

Answer is at the back of the book.

Little squares for dragon doodles

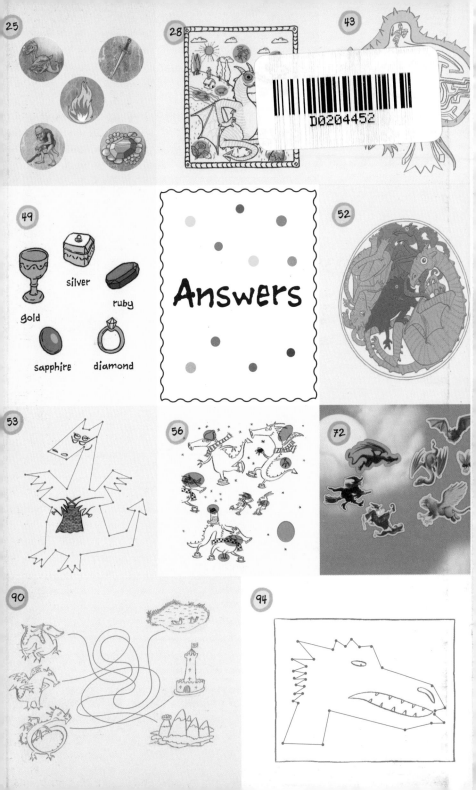

25

28

43

49

gold

silver

ruby

sapphire

diamond

Answers

52

53

56

72

90

94